ARCTIC OCEAN

Siberia

Scandinavia

Russia

ASIA

EUROPE

Japan

Himalayan Mts.

China

Israel

Egypt

AFRICA

Arabia

India

INDIAN OCEAN

AUSTRALIA

ANTARCTICA

YOU ARE HERE

A First Book of Places

By Michael Berenstain

A GOLDEN BOOK • NEW YORK

Western Publishing Company, Inc., Racine, Wisconsin 53404

Look!
We are here—right
here on the globe.
This is where we live.

We live in our own hometown.
We know our way around our hometown.

But what about outside our town?
What lies beyond the hills, far away?

We do not know. But we can find out.

We can find out in our You-Are-Here helicopter.

Now we can see far over the hills.

We can see bridges and streams, woods and farms. We can see the next town.

Can we see more?

7

Yes, we can!
Now we can see lakes and rivers,
mountains and big cities. We can see the
ocean. We can see the whole state!
Can we see even more?

Yes, we can!
Now we can see
our whole country,
the United States
of America—the
U.S.A.!
Let's drop in on
some of the most
famous places in
the U.S.A.

In the Black Hills of South Dakota, the faces of four Presidents are carved on Mount Rushmore. Can you name them?*

It took the Colorado River millions of years to dig out the Grand Canyon in Arizona.

*George Washington, Thomas Jefferson

The Statue of Liberty is on an island in New York City's harbor. She stands for freedom everywhere.

Way down south in Louisiana, steamboats sail on the Mississippi River.

The U.S.A. is a big place. Some parts of it are very far away.

Alaska, the most northern state, is the home of many Eskimos. They know how to build igloos—shelters made of snow.

Hawaii is a chain of islands in the Pacific Ocean. Here it is warm and sunny all year round.

We have now seen many places in the U.S.A. But what about other places in the world? Can we see other countries, too?

Yes, we can! But to see them we must first cross the ocean.
We will cross the wide Atlantic Ocean.

Canada

U.S.A.

EUROPE

ATLANTIC OCEAN

AFRICA

SOUTH AMERICA

Ireland

England

The Netherland

France

Spain

ATLANTIC OCEAN

On the other side of the ocean lies the continent of Europe. It is made up of many different countries. We can visit some of them.

England is part of an island. Its biggest city is London. We can check the time on the tall tower clock, Big Ben.

There is another famous tower, in Paris, the capital of France. The Eiffel Tower is very high. Let's fly around it.

In Madrid, Spain, we can
try our hands at bullfighting.
It's not so easy.
Look out!
The Leaning Tower of Pisa
is in Pisa, Italy. It almost looks
like it will fall over!

Far to the cold north is Russia, part of the Soviet Union, the world's biggest country. Its capital is Moscow. The tops of its old churches are shaped like onions. What are they called? Why, onion domes, of course.

Even farther north we come to the frozen Arctic Ocean. Here it is very, very cold. This is where the North Pole lies. The mysterious northern lights flicker in the sky.

Brrr! It's cold! Let's head south to warm up.

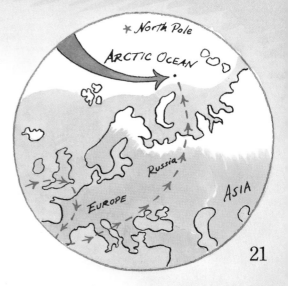

Black Sea

Down we go
into the continent of
Asia—home of many
ancient nations.

ASIA

Israel

Israel is the land of
many biblical cities,
including Jerusalem
and Bethlehem.

India has many
beautiful palaces.
Here we could ride
on an elephant.

Red Sea

Saudi
Arabia

India

Saudi Arabia is a
desert land. Oil wells
dot the sands. Much
of the world's oil is
found here.

AFRICA

INDIAN OCEAN

Siberia

China has more
people than any other
country. The Great Wall
of China was built long
ago to keep enemies out.

Japan

Korea

China

Japan is an
island country.
Its highest
mountain is
Fuji, an old
volcano.

Vietnam

Thailand

The Philippines

In Thailand
great temples
rise from the
jungle.

Borneo

Next door to the deserts of Asia lies the Sahara, a great desert of Africa.

The river Nile winds through this desert in the land of Egypt—the oldest country on Earth. Here pyramids and statues built in ancient times are still standing.

In the middle of the continent of Africa there are great jungles and plains, the home of many tropical animals—lions, giraffes, baboons, elephants, and rhinos.

To the south and east, across the Indian Ocean, lies Australia, both a country and a continent. Australia is a land of many strange animals. Here we can pet a koala and feed a kangaroo.

Even farther south, at the bottom of the world, we reach the continent of Antarctica. This is where the South Pole is found. It is the coldest place on Earth. No one lives on the land here except scientists and, of course, penguins.

Let's warm up again
by going north into the
continent of South America.

On the plains of Argentina,
gauchos catch large birds
called rheas for their feathers.
They catch them with bolas—
balls tied on the ends of strings.

In Brazil, the Amazon River flows through the world's largest jungle. The Amazon jungle is home to jaguars, tapirs with piglike snouts, giant snakes, crocodiles, and the capybara—a 100-pound rodent.

Above South America lies our own continent of North America. Here we can visit our neighbors in Mexico. It's fun to try and break the piñata at a Mexican birthday party.

U.S.A.

Mexico

Our other neighbor, Canada, is to our north. This is a country of great beauty—tall mountains, vast forests, and sparkling lakes.

Next we come to . . .
the U.S.A. again!

We are right here—right back in
our own hometown.

Now we know our way around the
whole world!

If you want to see all the places we
have been, just turn the page.

Alaska

The Rockies

Greenland

NORTH AMERICA

Canada

U.S.A.

Engla

Mexico

ATLANTIC OCEAN

SP

Sah

Hawaii

PACIFIC OCEAN

The Andes

SOUTH AMERICA

Brazil

Argentina

YOU ARE HERE